For Grandma and Grandpa Rothman.

– Roselyn Kasmire

PRT0515A

Printed in the United States

Library of Congress Control Number: 2015900921
ISBN-13: 978-1-62086-937-6

www.mascotbooks.com

Mage Magnus
and the
Curse of Frogitoo

Roselyn Kasmire
Illustrated by Mike Alvarez

M

age Magnus was excited to get to magic school. Before he left the house he grabbed his lucky wand and stuck his pet toad in his pocket.

He even gave his mom a kiss on the cheek before he left.

He opened his window and swung
down the ivy along his house.

He went into his backyard and unleashed his pet dragon, Sparks.

Sparks flew so high, Mage could see the top of the mountains covered in snow.

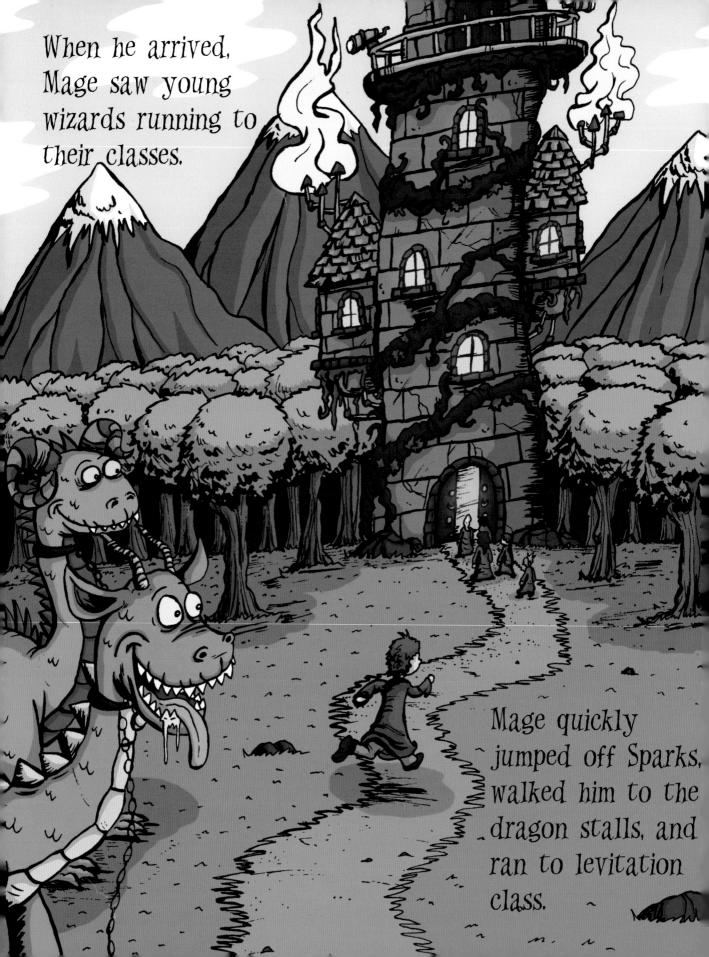

When he arrived, Mage saw young wizards running to their classes.

Mage quickly jumped off Sparks, walked him to the dragon stalls, and ran to levitation class.

The professor of levitation was waiting at the front of the room as the students came in and took their seats.

Mage was the last student to arrive. As he rushed to an empty seat, he overheard Alda telling another student, "This is where we'll learn to make things float in the air!"

I can't wait! I'll never have to pick up a mess in my room again! I can make a broom sweep without actually sweeping. I'm going to love this class! thought Mage.

The professor began class. "Good morning, students. My name is Professor Levitora. Are you ready to learn some magic?"

"Yes!" replied the class.

"The spell I'm going to teach you today is called, 'Levoootaaah.' Class, watch very carefully the way I control my wand. I'm going to make this desk fly around the room."

Levitora slowly picked up her wand and said the magic word, "Levoootaaah!" The desk rose slowly as she controlled it with her wand. The students were hypnotized in amazement as their eyes followed the desk. Then, it softly landed back where it started.

"Now, class, it's your turn. Let's see what you young wizards can do. We'll start with the basics. Pick something small and make it levitate." All the students pointed their wands at different things in the classroom.

Mage Magnus spotted a toy wazoolo on Professor Levitora's desk. Mage pointed his wand at the wazoolo then shouted, "Leevooote!"

All of a sudden, the wazoolo came to life and jumped onto Professor Levitora's head! Then it started running around the room, jumping from desk to desk, making papers fall, and screaming and laughing all the while. The wazoolo was such a distraction, the young wizards lost their concentration and couldn't practice the spell.

Professor Levitora tried to catch the wazoolo, but the toy was too fast and ran into a mouse hole in the wall.

"Okay, class. That will be enough for today. Tomorrow you'll try the spell again," said Professor Levitora.

All the other students were upset they couldn't practice. Mage Magnus was so embarrassed. He sat at his desk as the students left the classroom. Mage was the last to leave. He went to the courtyard and overheard some of his classmates making fun of him.

He felt so bad already, but the other young wizards kept making fun of his mistake.

One young wizard named Elmer told Mage, "I don't know why you're here. All you do is make mistakes. One day we'll be great and you'll still be in magic school. You can't do anything right. Just go home."

Mage was so upset he pointed his wand at Elmer and screamed the first thing that came to his mind. "Frogitoo!" Elmer froze and shrunk into a toad.
All the students in the courtyard started to scream.

Ozard, sleeping in his oak, was awakened.

He opened his eyes and saw a bunch of students in a circle.

Ozard stretched his wings and flew down to see what the ruckus was. He landed in the middle of the circle.

"Well, Mage turned Elmer into a toad," said Zera.

"Is that true, Mage?" asked Ozard.

"Yes, but he was making fun of me. He made me feel so bad about myself I couldn't let him get away with it. So I turned him into a toad," responded Mage.

"I see. Well, I will reverse the spell on Elmer and we'll discuss what to do," said Ozard.

Ozard put his grey, feathery wing over Elmer's head and hooted, "Unfrogitoo!"

Elmer changed back into
a young wizard.

Elmer yelled at Mage, "You turned me into a toad! I'm going to turn you into a toad and see how you like it!"

"Silence!" squawked Ozard. "You two young wizards need to talk this out. What both of you did was wrong. Elmer, why did you make fun of Mage when he made a mistake? Was that being a good wizard?"

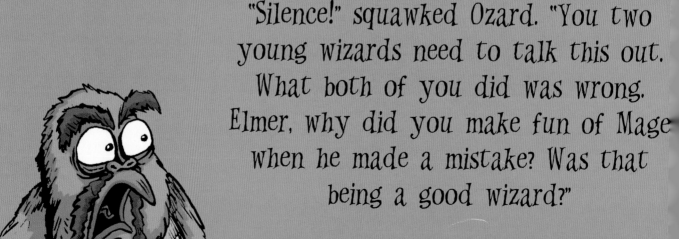

"I guess not," said Elmer, "but he always makes mistakes and he made us miss our class. It takes away the time we have to learn new magic."

"Elmer, making fun of Mage and hurting his feelings is bullying," responded Ozard.

"What's a bully?" asked Mage.

"A bully picks on other people to make themselves feel better. They don't care about the other person's feelings. Elmer, you were being a bully," responded Ozard.

"No I wasn't! Mage was!" replied Elmer. "He's the one who turned me into a toad!"

"Yes, but you made me feel bad about myself and my feelings were hurt. I thought I had no other choice," said Mage.

"Well, I'm sorry I made you feel that way. I should have been a better wizard and asked you if you needed help with your spells instead of saying all those mean things to you."

Ozard turned to Mage and said, "Mage, what you did to Elmer was not nice either. You shouldn't have used your magic to turn Elmer into a toad. If Elmer made you upset, you should have told him. Then if he continued making fun of you, you should have talked to the Great Wizard about it."

Elmer said, "I'm sorry, Mage. I didn't know you felt bad about what happened in class. I thought you didn't care and it was a joke to you. I can help you after magic school with your spells."

"I would really like that, and I'm sorry for turning you into a toad," said Mage.

"I guess my job here is done!" Ozard hooted. He spread his wings and flew back to the great oak tree.

Suddenly, Elmer and Mage heard girls screaming. They turned and saw the wazoolo jumping on the girls' heads while laughing and singing. Elmer and Mage looked at each other, and Elmer asked...

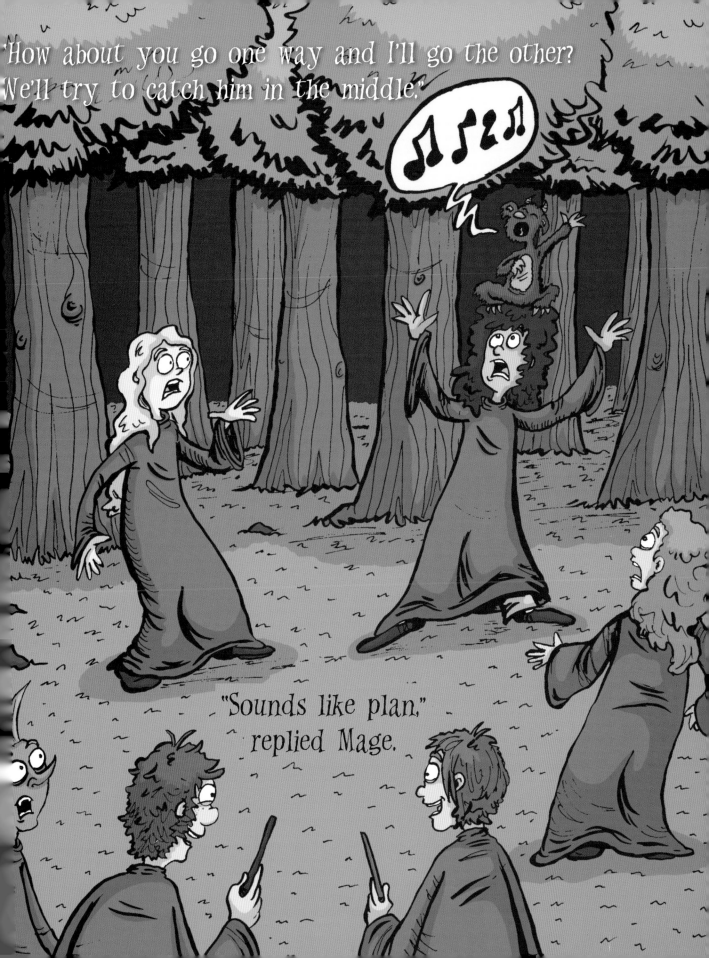

Also Available...
The Misadventures of
Mage Magnus

Coming soon...
The Misadventures of
Mage Magnus:
The Magical Mistake

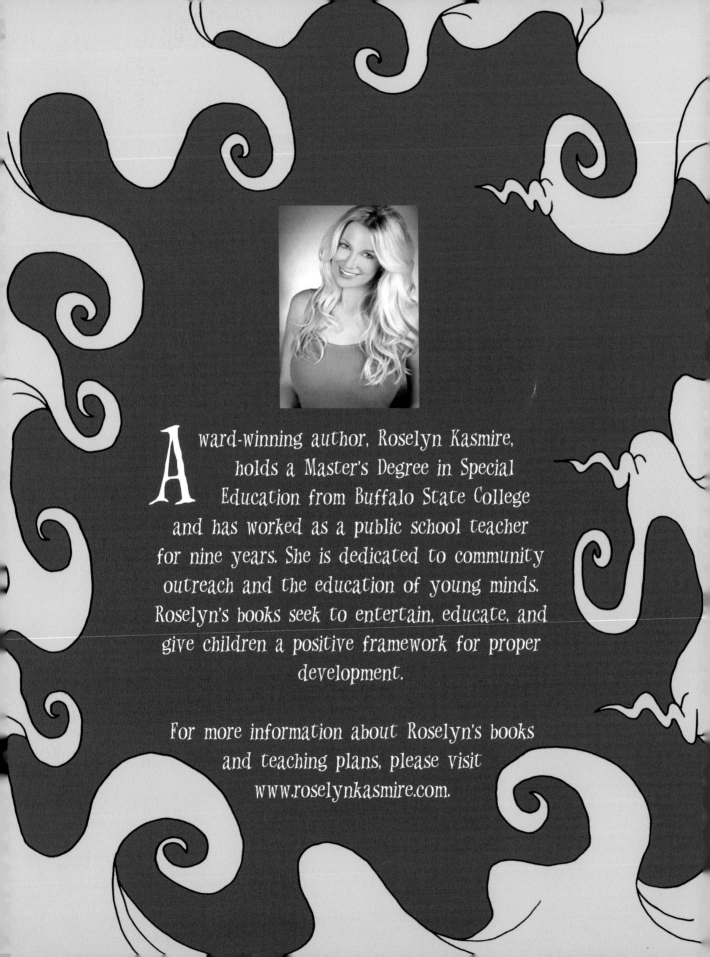

Award-winning author, Roselyn Kasmire, holds a Master's Degree in Special Education from Buffalo State College and has worked as a public school teacher for nine years. She is dedicated to community outreach and the education of young minds. Roselyn's books seek to entertain, educate, and give children a positive framework for proper development.

For more information about Roselyn's books and teaching plans, please visit www.roselynkasmire.com.